This Is the House That Was Tidy & Neat

Teri Sloat ∽ illustrated by R.W. Alley

Henry Holt and Company ∽ New York

Henry Holt and Company, LLC
Publishers since 1866
115 West 18th Street
New York, New York 10011
www.henryholt.com

Library of Congress Cataloging-in-Publication Data
Sloat, Teri.
This is the house that was tidy and neat / Teri Sloat; illustrated by R. W. Alley.—1st ed.
p.   cm.
Summary: After a series of mishaps involving crumbs, drips, splatters,
and spills, the neat and tidy house that Mom left is a mess.
ISBN-13: 978-0-8050-6921-1 / ISBN-10: 0-8050-6921-6
[1. Cleanliness—Fiction. 2. Orderliness—Fiction. 3. Stories in rhyme.] I. Alley, R. W. (Robert W.), ill. II. Title.
PZ8.3.S63245Tj 2005   [E]—dc22   2004010133

First Edition—2005
Printed in the United States of America on acid-free paper. ∞

1 3 5 7 9 10 8 6 4 2

The artist used pen and ink and watercolors on Strathmore paper to create the illustrations for this book.

To my husband, who cooks while I put up my feet,
and to those who keep houses tidy and neat

−T. S.

This is the house . . .

. . . At the end of the street
That was tidy and neat
When Mom left.

This is the mouse

Who lives in the wall

Twitching his whiskers

And watching crumbs fall

In the cozy old house

At the end of the street

That was tidy and neat

When Mom left.

This is the cat

Who prowls through the house

Switching his tail,

Sneaking up on the mouse

Who nibbles on crumbs

He's been waiting to eat

On the floor of the house

At the end of the street

That was tidy and neat

When Mom left.

This is the dog
Who stands dripping wet
Outside the back door,
Just waiting to get
The cat who is sneaking
Up on the mouse
Who nibbles on crumbs
On the floor of the house
At the end of the street
That was tidy and neat
When Mom left.

This is the boy
Who opens the door
And lets in the dog
Who slides 'cross the floor

And barks at the cat

Who chases the mouse

Who nibbles on crumbs

That fell in the house

At the end of the street

That was tidy and neat

When Mom left.

This is the girl
Who suddenly spills
The milk as she misses
The glass that she fills,

And blames the boy
Who opened the door
And let in the dog
Who barked at the cat
Who chased the mouse
Who nibbles on crumbs . . .

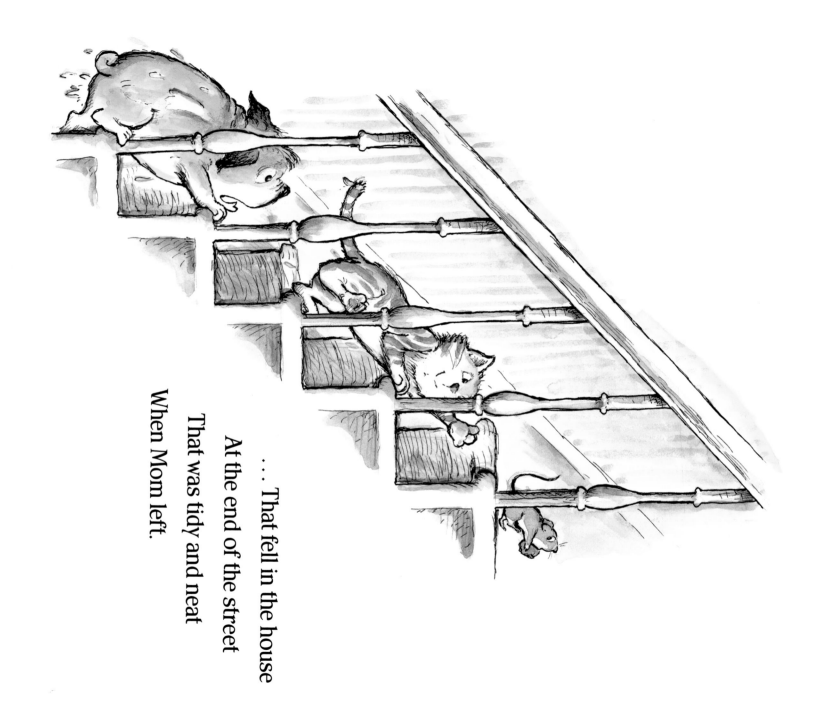

. . . That fell in the house
At the end of the street
That was tidy and neat
When Mom left.

This is the nanny
Who dropped off to sleep
And was snoring away . . .

. . . Forgetting to keep
An eye on the girl
Who spilled all the milk
And blamed the boy
Who opened the door
And let in the dog
Who barked at the cat
Who chased the mouse
Who nibbles on crumbs
That fell in the house
At the end of the street . . .

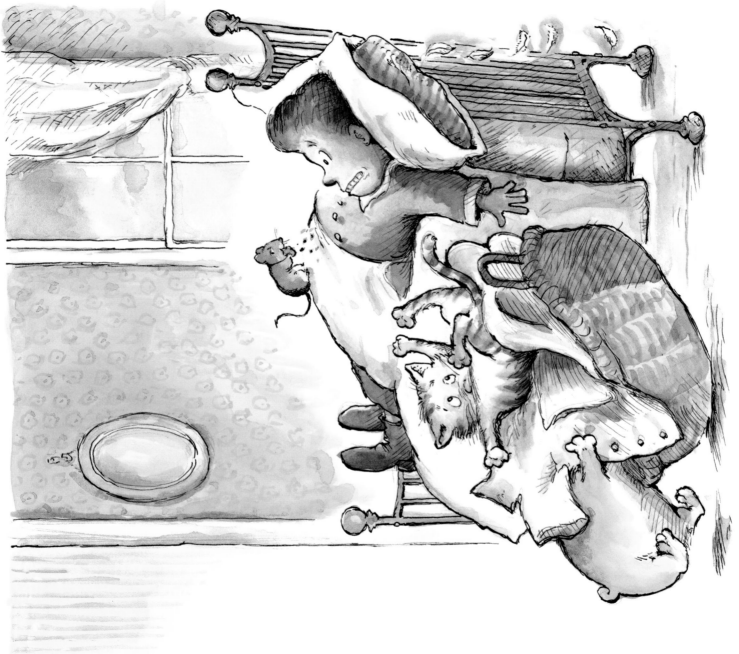

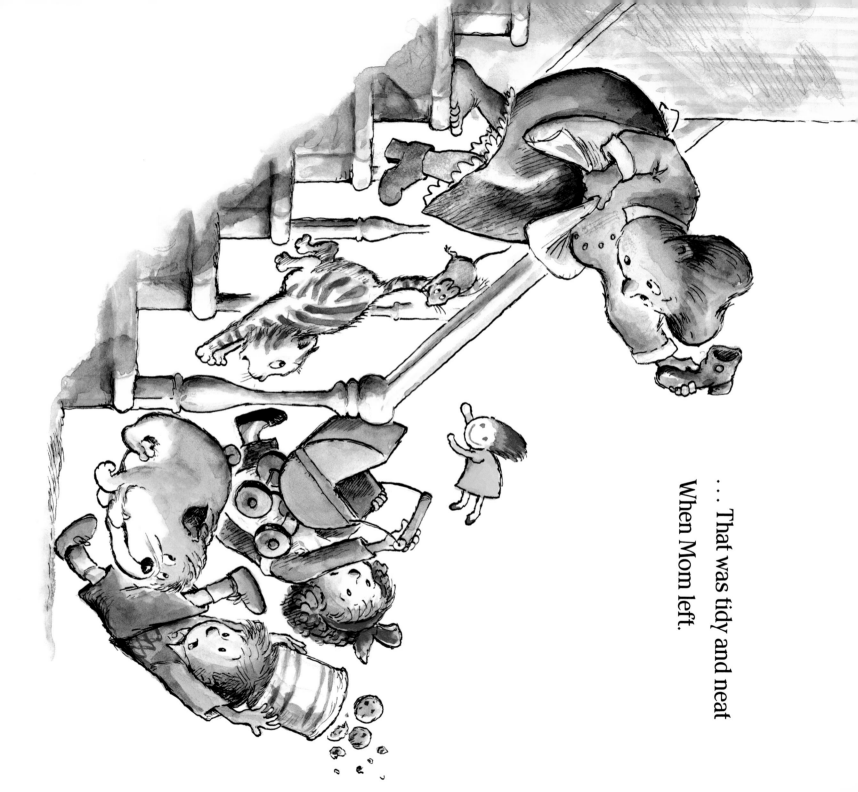

... That was tidy and neat
When Mom left.

This is the dad
Coming home for the night
Who opens the door
To the house . . .

... *What a sight!*

He hurries to mop
The milk from the floor

While Nanny wipes down
The table and door,

And the girl cleans splatters
Of milk from the wall
And the boy scrubs away
The tracks from the hall,

And lets out the dog

Who barked at the cat

Who chased the mouse

Who hides in the house

At the end of the street

That was tidy and neat

When Mom left.

This is the mom

Coming home up the street . . .

. . . Who sinks in a chair
And puts up her feet

And rests while the dad
Fixes something to eat . . .

. . . In the cozy old house

At the end of the street

That is tidy and neat

When Mom's home.